*In memory of
my father*

Copyright © 1993 by Kim Lewis

First U.S. edition 1993
Published in Great Britain in 1993 by Walker Books Ltd., London.

ISBN 1-56402-194-7

Library of Congress Catalog Card Number 92-54413
Library of Congress Cataloging-in-Publication Data is available.

10 9 8 7 6 5 4 3 2 1

Printed in Hong Kong

The pictures in this book were done in colored pencils.

Candlewick Press
2067 Massachusetts Avenue
Cambridge, Massachusetts 02140

# First Snow

# KIM LEWIS

CANDLEWICK PRESS
CAMBRIDGE, MASSACHUSETTS

"Wake up, Sara," whispered Mommy. "Daddy's not very well today. I'm going to feed the sheep on the hill. Would you and Teddy like to come?"

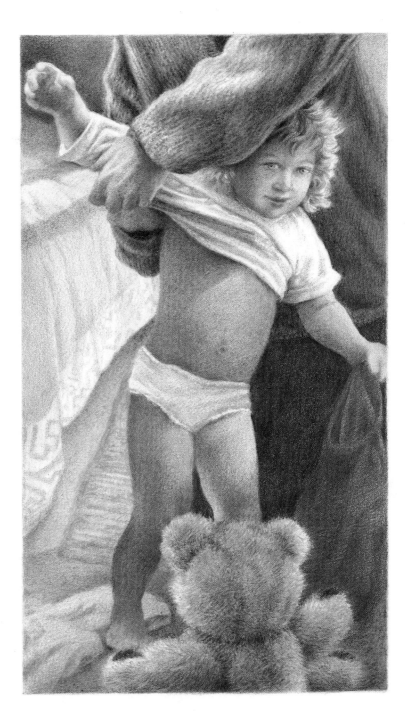

Outside the dogs
were ready and waiting,
bright-eyed and eager to go.
Frost nipped the air. It was
early winter and the rooks
were calling. A wind was
starting to blow.

Through the gate and
up the steep path,
Mommy and Sara climbed.
The sky turned grayer and
the air grew colder.
The dogs raced on ahead.
As they climbed higher,
Sara looked back.
The farmhouse seemed
very small.

At the top of the hill stood the lone pine tree, bent by years of winter winds. Mommy and Sara stopped below it to rest. The air went suddenly still. "We're on top of the world," said Mommy, hugging Sara. "Just you and me and Teddy."

Across the valley the sky turned white.

Snowflakes lightly danced in the air.

"Look, look!" Sara laughed.

She watched as a snowflake fell on her mitten.

"We'd better feed the sheep," said Mommy,

"before it snows too hard."

Sara helped Mommy spread hay on the ground. The sheep were hungry and pushed all around them. Sara tried catching the snow in her hands, but the wind swirled the snowflakes in front of her eyes.

Then the snow fell faster
and stung Sara's cheeks.
The air grew thick and white.
"Come on," said Mommy,
her hand out to Sara.
"The sheep are all right and
we must go home before
the snow gets too deep."

The dogs disappeared through the flying snow.

Snow blotted out the lone pine.

Mommy and Sara started down the path,

hugging close to the wall.

Then suddenly Sara stopped.

"Oh no, where's Teddy?" she cried.

Mommy looked back.
Behind them the snow
was filling their tracks.
"We can't look for Teddy
now," said Mommy.
She whistled for the dogs
and started to walk, but
Sara sat still in the snow.

Then out of the whiteness,

one of the dogs appeared.

She was gently carrying Teddy.

"Oh, Teddy," cried Sara,

hugging him tight.

Mommy picked up Sara and

Teddy.

"Now we can all go home,"

she said.

As they came down the hill, the air cleared
of snow. The sky began turning blue.
Sara and Mommy could see the farmhouse
again, standing snug in the yard.
The world all around them was white and still.

Sara and Mommy
warmed up by the fire.
Then they took Daddy
his breakfast in bed.
"Who's fed the sheep?"
Daddy asked them.
Sara snuggled up
beside him.
"Mommy and Teddy
and me!" she said.